Lost!

A True Tale from the Bush

Stephanie Owen Reeder

National Library of Australia

To my three intrepid children—may you always return home safely from your adventures! SOR

Published by the National Library of Australia
Canberra   ACT   2600

National Library of Australia Cataloguing-in-Publication entry
Author: Reeder, Stephanie Owen.
Title: Lost!:a true tale from the bush / Stephanie Owen Reeder.
ISBN: 9780642276865 (hbk.)
Target Audience: For primary school age.
Subjects: Frontier and pioneer life--Victoria--Juvenile literature.
             Tracking and trailing--Juvenile literature.
             Children's clothing--Victoria--History--19th century.
             Education--Victoria--History--19th century.
             Toys--Victoria--History--19th century.
Other Authors/Contributors:
Strutt, William, 1825-1915 Cooey.
Dewey Number: 994.5031

Project Manager: Susan Hall
Editor: Joanna Karmel
Designers: Cate Eggleton, Lindsay Davidson and Noel Wendtman
Printed in China by Australian Book Connection

Cover image: William Strutt (1825–1915), *The Little Wanderers* 1865 (see page 109)
Back cover image: Sarah Stone (1760–1844), *Snake; Muricated Lizard* 1790 (see page 105)

CONTENTS

INTRODUCTION

In the winter of 1864, three young children—Isaac, nine, Jane, seven, and Frank, nearly four—were lost in the bush near Natimuk in the Wimmera District of Victoria for nine long days and eight cold nights.

The Duff children's amazing adventure captured the public's imagination, and it was widely covered in newspapers and magazines of the time.

This miraculous tale of perseverance and love also inspired authors, artists and film-makers. William Strutt, an English illustrator who lived in Australia for a number of years, was completely entranced by the story. Some years after the event, he wrote a fictionalised, somewhat didactic and sometimes inaccurate version. However, it was accompanied by beautiful watercolour paintings. His manuscript and illustrations are held in the

National Library of Australia, and the Library published a facsimile edition, *Cooey, or, The Trackers of Glenferry*, in 1989.

Lost! A True Tale from the Bush was inspired by Strutt's story and features his illustrations. However, in this version, details of the children's ordeal and the ongoing search for them are mainly based on eyewitness and newspaper accounts. Other retellings written over the years have also been consulted. As often happens, each retelling has been embellished in some way to bring the story to life, and *Lost!* is no different. However, as far as possible, this is a historically accurate reconstruction of the children's incredible journey. As well as the story itself, there is an informative section at the end of each chapter that gives insights into how children lived in the 1860s.

Isaac practised his cooeeing in the mallee-tree forest.

CHAPTER 1
Mallee Monsters and Wildflowers

Friday, 12 August 1864

'I'm hungry!' Frankie mumbled, half asleep, as Jane slipped out of the bed she shared with him and her older brother, Isaac. She pulled her favourite dress over her head and then tied on her white apron. She could hear the magpies warbling their morning song as she tiptoed over

Jane's mother had put the damper on the fire to cook.

to the fireplace. Her mother, Hannah Duff, was raking the coals to get the fire going for breakfast.

'Morning, poppet. Could you fetch some water, please?'

Jane headed out the door, collecting the heavy bucket on the way. She struggled to carry it, even empty, for Jane was only seven. She coughed as the cold air of the late winter morning hit her lungs. After ladling water from the barrel into the bucket, Jane wrestled it back inside, the water sloshing over her boots.

Inside their one-room slab hut, Jane's mother had put the damper in the camp oven to cook. Jane stuck her nose over the heavy iron pot sitting on the flames and inhaled the mouth-watering baking smells. The tea was brewing and mutton chops sizzled on a griddle nearby. She screwed up her nose—more tough old meat from the tough old sheep that her father had killed last week.

Jane wished they could have something tastier,
like the scrumptious parrot pie they had had for her
birthday. But then she remembered crying when she
saw her mother plucking the brilliantly coloured feathers
from the dead birds.

After she set the table with their tin plates and mugs,
she walked to the back of the room and peeled the blanket
off her brothers. 'Wake up, sleepy heads!'

Isaac, who was two years older than Jane, hated
mornings. He grumbled as he swung his legs over the side
of the mattress and pulled on his
clothes. Then he dunked his head
into a bucket of cold water, and came
up a little less grumpy.

Frankie was nearly four, but Jane still
helped him to get dressed, wriggling him
into his pantaloons and tugging his dress
down firmly over his head. Frankie was not old
enough to wear short pants, but he didn't care.

*Jane could hear the
magpies warbling.*

Frankie babbled away about monsters that lived in the mallee-tree forest.

He was his usual bright, cheeky self, babbling away about monsters that lived in the mallee-tree forest.

Their father, John Duff, sat at the head of the table and said a quick prayer before the family ate. After breakfast, he set off for work, riding his horse to Spring Hill Station, where he was a carpenter and shepherd.

While Jane helped their mother clear the table, the boys rolled their mattress into a corner, making a game of it.

'We've got the big mallee monster! Don't let him escape!' Frankie yelled, struggling to keep his footing as the mattress got away from him.

'Come on, you two,' their mother said, 'you boys still have more chores to do. This broom is starting to break apart. I need more twigs from the heath in the forest—you know the broombushes I mean. Off you go.'

'Please, can Jane come too?' Isaac begged. 'I want to show her the paper daisies near the broombush scrub.'

'All right, you can all go, but take your hats.' And she sent them on their way with treacle sandwiches wrapped

in a cloth and a stern warning to take care and not be
late home.

'We'll be back in plenty of time for tea,' Jane promised
solemnly.

The children marched into the forest. It was a scrubby
place, full of stunted, twisted mallee trees. Their leafy
canopy provided shelter for passing echidnas and possums.
Saltbush, tea-trees, heath and wattle grew amongst them,
as well as prickly porcupine grass—a perfect hiding place
for snakes. Isaac led the way, armed with his tomahawk
and twirling a walking stick he had made from a stout
wattle branch.

'That's where we're going,' said Isaac, pointing to a
slight rise in the distance. 'I'll race you there,' he yelled,
as he dashed off. Jane hitched up her dress and set off
after him at a sprint, her apron strings and bonnet ribbons
trailing in her wake.

Jane caught up with Isaac and they collapsed amongst
the wildflowers, laughing and out of breath. Frankie soon

The forest was a scrubby place, full of stunted, twisted mallee trees.

appeared, his dress bunched up around his waist, his short legs pumping hard, and a scowl on his little red face.

'You didn't wait!' he bellowed.

Jane gave him a quick hug and tucked a flower behind his ear.

Frankie threw the flower on the ground. A movement near his foot caught his eye and he was soon totally absorbed in chasing lizards. Jane picked a bunch of flowers for her mother and then made a wreath out of paper daisies, tying it around her bonnet.

'Hey, you two, there's a really good clump of broombush just over that fence,' Isaac shouted from halfway up a tree. 'Let's go and collect some.'

They soon had three large bunches of twigs, so they sat down under a wattle tree and ate their sandwiches.

The leafy canopy provided shelter for passing echidnas.

A blue-tongue lizard ambled by and a flock of red-eyed choughs bustled about in the leaf litter.

'I'm still hungry,' Frankie declared.

'You're always hungry! Here, have some of this.' Isaac peeled some resinous gum from the wattle tree and handed it to Frankie. He licked it and a smile lit up his face.

'It's sweet!' he chortled, and he had soon devoured the lot. The children lay back in the wattle's shade and watched the passing parade of clouds.

'We'd better get home soon or Mother will get worried,' Jane said, hopping to her feet and brushing wattle blossom from her dress.

Off the three children set, the bundles of broombush tucked under their arms. Frankie was tired, hungry and cranky, so Jane took his hand and chatted to him, while Isaac practised his cooeeing, the distinctive sound echoing through the surrounding bush.

SLAB HUTS, TIN TUBS AND CHAMBER POTS: HOUSING IN THE 1860s

Huts in the bush were made from slabs of wood.

Wealthy people built solid houses from bricks and stones in the 1860s. However, most families in the bush made their homes from whatever materials they could find. They used whole logs or slabs of roughly cut wood held together by wooden pegs. Wattle-and-daub houses were also popular. They cut down wattle-tree branches, wove them together and then covered them with mud or clay, using bark or wooden shingles for the roof.

People made ceilings out of canvas, and pasted newspaper onto the walls to keep out the heat and the cold. The floor was dirt—people stamped on it to make it hard. They sewed kangaroo skins around the doorframes to keep the wind and the cold from seeping through the gaps around the door. Huts usually had only one room, so the family made 'rooms' by hanging blankets over ropes. The fireplace was the centre of home life.

Slab huts usually had only one room.

Houses had no electricity, so there were no lights, fridges or TVs.

Families in the bush didn't have the home comforts that we take for granted. There was no electricity, so they didn't have lights, fridges or stoves. The children slept together in one bed—usually a mattress on the floor or a stretcher their father had made. Their mother sewed together possum skins, flour bags or patchwork squares to make blankets. And she washed their clothes in the creek or in a tub.

Huts had no running water and no toilet.

Children fetched water from the creek, river or dam. It was stored in a large barrel near their hut. They washed their faces and hands in a basin or went swimming in the creek. Occasionally, they had a good scrub in a large tin tub, using soap their mothers had made. They cleaned their teeth with the frayed end of a twig dipped in bicarbonate of soda mixed with chalk. Toilets were either chamber pots that were kept under the beds or holes dug outside. As candles were expensive, families often went to bed at sunset.

The children's cooees and cries of 'Mother!', 'Father!' echoed through the bush.

CHAPTER 2
Kookaburras and Cooees

Friday, 12 August 1864

'Mother's making kangaroo stew for tea. I can't wait. Come on, this way,' Isaac said confidently. As the children scrambled through the maze of mallee trees, Frankie's stomach rumbled loudly.

'Come on, short legs. We'll never get home at this rate,' Isaac encouraged him. 'We should come to that fence shortly.'

On they tramped, glancing from side to side. Isaac was very relieved when they finally came upon a fence.

'See, I knew we'd find it,' he crowed. 'We'll soon be home and eating that kangaroo stew!'

But the further they walked, the more unfamiliar the countryside looked. Isaac's face wore an anxious expression as he scanned the scrub.

'I'll just climb this tree. I'm sure I'll see home from there,' he said, afraid to admit he was totally bamboozled.

From his perch, Isaac scoured the landscape, but all he could see was a vast carpet of treetops. There were no comforting wisps of smoke from a chimney; no sound of the bells of cattle or bullocks; no bleating of sheep or neighing of horses.

Isaac rubbed a tear from his eye. How was he going to tell Frankie and Jane that they were lost? He was their big

The further the children walked, the more unfamiliar the countryside looked.

brother, and mother trusted him to look
after them.

'I'm sorry, but I think we've come
the wrong way,' he mumbled, as he
reached the ground.

'We can't be far from home,' Jane said. 'We just
have to cooee really loudly and Mother will hear us.'

The children's cooees and cries of 'Mother!',
'Father!' echoed through the bush, but the only response
was the screaming cacophony of a flock of cockatoos,
the rattle of gum leaves in the rising wind and the cackle
of a kookaburra that had just caught a snake. Frankie
began to cry.

'Here, Isaac will take your broombush and I'll hold your
hand,' Jane said, trying to cheer him up. 'I'm sure Mother
will be so relieved to see us when we get home that she'll
let us have some Black Jack as a special treat.'

Frankie's eyes lit up at the thought of the brown sugar
he loved so much.

The only response was the cackle of a kookaburra that had just caught a snake.

As darkness descended, a dingo howled in the distance.
The children huddled together under the golden canopy of
a wattle tree. They took off their boots and socks, as they
did every night, and put their arms around each other.

The nocturnal bush creatures began to wake up.
A curlew cried as it emerged from its nest under a fallen log;
a possum blundered around in a nearby tree; and a quoll,
its white spots reflecting in the moonlight, scavenged for
insects and small animals to eat.

'What's that?' whispered Frankie, fear in his voice.

'It's just a wild cat looking for his tea,' said Jane.

Isaac, trying to steer the conversation away from things
that might devour them in the

*A quoll, its white
spots reflecting in the
moonlight, scavenged
for insects.*

night, began to chat about what they might do when they were back home.

'Let's finish that game of snakes and ladders we started last night. And I'll even play Chinese checkers with you, Jane, even though you always win! Maybe Mother will finish that story she was reading to us—the one about the poor little match girl out in the snow.'

Jane shivered. She looked around for something to cover them with, but the only thing she could think of was her dress. So she took it off and lay down on the hard ground in her petticoats. Frankie was sandwiched warmly between his brother and sister, with Jane's dress draped over him. They snuggled together and sobbed themselves to sleep.

It was late afternoon and, in the little hut on the edge of the mallee scrub, Hannah Duff sat sewing a dress for Jane. In and out her needle darted. Every now and then she looked up and cocked her head, thinking she could hear the children's voices. As evening came, she put her sewing aside, went outside and shouted over and over, 'Isaac! Jane! Frankie!'. But there was no reply. She grabbed her shawl and set off for the patch of broombush, where she cooeed until she was hoarse. When she returned to the hut, the children still had not returned.

At sunset, John Duff rode in from work. Hannah rushed into his arms, pouring out the story of the children's disappearance.

'Don't worry. They'll be all right. I'll find them,' he reassured her. He set off at once, zigzagging on foot through the scrub, searching for the children's trail, shouting their names and cooeeing loudly. There were no answering calls.

'I'll go to the homestead and get a search party together,' John Duff told his wife as he galloped away on his horse to raise the alarm.

In no time at all, a posse of men had gathered, their horses snorting and pawing the ground, eager to start.

They quickly reached the broombush patch and searched by the light of the full moon—the same moon that, some miles away, bathed the sleeping children in its light.

'I'm sure we'll find them before the moon sets,' John Duff declared.

Meanwhile, the children's mother kept herself busy. She set the table, brewed the tea and put the kangaroo stew on the fire to simmer. Then she sat staring into the flames, the book she had been reading to the children the night before open on her lap. Every so often, a tear dropped onto the page.

At the sound of a horse cantering into the yard, Hannah ran outside, but only disappointment met her, for John Duff's arms were empty.

The search party quickly reached the broombush patch and searched by the light of the full moon.

CIRCUSES, BUSHRANGERS AND BATTLEDORE: CHILDREN'S ENTERTAINMENT IN THE 1860s

Children loved playing ball games like cricket.

In the 1860s, there weren't any televisions, DVDs, or electronic games and so children had to entertain themselves. They played blind man's bluff, hide-and-seek, cricket and other ball games. They climbed trees, built cubby houses and looked for birds' nests. They also picked flowers to make daisy-chain necklaces and crowns, caught butterflies and cicadas in nets, or fished for eels and yabbies.

Children in the bush loved the freedom of playing outdoors. They played games of hopscotch and battledore (a game like badminton), or pretended to be bushrangers. They also had lots of chores, such as chopping wood, carting water or helping with the cleaning and baking. But when they had spare time, they climbed trees and swam in creeks and waterholes.

Make-believe games, like playing bushrangers, were popular.

Not many families owned books. Mothers recited rhymes that they had learnt from their mothers. If there were books in the house, they were probably Bible stories, the fairytales of Hans Christian Andersen and tales especially for children about the dangers of foolish behaviour. The first book for children published in Australia was *A Mother's Offering to Her Children* (1841), a dull story about courage, hard work and honesty. The first Australian picture book (1862), was more fun. It was called *Who Killed Cockatoo?* and had black-and-white illustrations.

The first Australian picture book was called *Who Killed Cockatoo?*

Travelling circuses sometimes visited country areas. Children loved the acrobats and trained animals, and the sideshows with 'freaks' such as bearded ladies and strongmen. Children also enjoyed the Punch and Judy puppet shows because they could boo the villain and cheer the heroes and heroines. But travelling shows didn't visit often, so they sat by the fire and played board games such as snakes and ladders, Chinese checkers and chess.

Children played board games on cold winter afternoons.

That evening the children huddled together, wet, cold and very miserable.

CHAPTER 3

Piggybacks and Quandongs

Jane opened one eye and then another. She closed them quickly when she realised where she was.

'Bother, it's not just a bad dream,' she muttered, as she looked out on the bleak bush surrounding her.

A kookaburra laughed and a hopping mouse paused, sniffed the air and then shot off into the underbrush.

'I'm hungry and I want my mother,' a little voice said nearby. Frankie was awake. His hair was tangled and his face was smeared with the sticky residue of wattle-tree gum.

Jane took a handful of her dress, spat on it and wiped his scowling face. She then put her dress back on and went looking for her stockings.

'Who's hidden my socks?' Isaac demanded, with his usual morning grumpiness. 'It's not funny!'

'It wasn't me,' said Jane. 'I can't find my stockings or Frankie's socks either!'

They looked in bushes, under logs and even in the porcupine grass. They found ants and spiders, lizards and flies, but they did not find their socks.

'Maybe that rotten wild cat stole them when it was creeping around here last night,' said Isaac.

'Well, I want them back! I'm not putting on my boots without my socks,' Frankie complained. But he had no choice.

The children, their throats dry with thirst, wandered through the scrub for some time, looking in vain for a creek or a billabong.

'Oh, Ike, what are we going to do?' asked Jane.

'I know! There should still be some dew on the leaves around here.' The children were very quiet for a while as they licked the moisture off gum leaves, one by one. Then, feeling a little refreshed, they clambered up a tree as far as they could and started to yell.

'Mother! Father! Cooeeeeee!'

'Maybe Father's not looking for us at the moment and has gone home to help Mother. It's Saturday after all and we're not there to help her with the chores,' said Jane, trying to explain the silence that answered their plaintive cries.

The children licked the moisture off gum leaves, one by one.

The children shed some tears. But they were more determined than ever to find their way home and so they ignored their aching limbs, rumbling stomachs, dry throats and the shoes chaffing their tired feet, and set off once again.

Isaac scaled another tree. 'We must be able to see Mount Arapiles. At least then we'll have some idea where we are.' But all he could see was more bush.

'My feet are sore and my tummy's rumbling and I'm not going any further!' Frankie announced, sitting down abruptly on a hollow log.

'We have to keep going, Frankie, or we'll never get home. Come on, I'll give you a piggyback.' Isaac crouched down and then hoisted the solid little boy onto his back.

'Giddy-up!' yelled Frankie, kicking his feet in the air, but the best Isaac could do was to plod along. He carefully placed one foot in front of the other as he negotiated the hazardous ground with its sharp-leaved bushes, fallen tree trunks, twisted mallee roots and sandy soil.

Jane looked out on the bleak bush surrounding her. A kookaburra laughed.

The children stopped near a large bush covered in red berries.

The children kept on walking until the sun was right above their heads. Hunger and thirst gnawed at them and Isaac's back ached from carrying Frankie. They stopped near a large bush covered in red berries.

'Food!' Frankie shouted triumphantly, stuffing the quandongs into his mouth. Jane and Isaac chewed more cautiously, not sure if the berries would do them more harm than good. The fruit was not quite ripe and it had a slightly bitter taste. Isaac spat his out.

'I'm sure I heard Father say these things are poisonous. Look at the colour—they look poisonous to me!'

'Are you sure he said that?' asked Jane, who had already swallowed a mouthful. Frankie just ignored them and kept eating, the juice dribbling down his chin.

'I'm sure!' said Isaac. 'If you eat any more you'll get stomach aches,' he declared. 'And then you'll get the runs, and there are no chamber pots out here!'

Jane reluctantly dropped a handful of berries. 'That's enough, Frankie. You'll get sick.'

'It's not fair. I'm hungry!' said Frankie, defiantly shovelling berries into his mouth until Isaac dragged him away. Isaac and Jane headed off again, chewing on grass stalks, while behind them Frankie happily munched on the last of his berries.

As the day wore on, the sky turned grey and rain began to fall. The children danced about in it, their mouths wide open, drinking in the welcome water, shouting with delight. But that evening they huddled together under a prickly tea-tree bush, wet, cold and very, very miserable.

'Cooee! Cooee!' John Duff called as he cantered on his horse into the homestead yard of Spring Hill Station at dawn that Saturday and rallied the men. The station manager was already up, organising a large search party. Bushmen came from neighbouring properties and soon there were more than 30 people on horseback and on foot searching for the missing children in the mallee scrub. But, like the day before, they did not find their trail. The men returned to the station that night, wet, weary and very, very worried.

All Isaac could see was more bush.

BUSH RATS, PARROT PIE AND POSSUMS: FOOD IN THE 1860s

Girls helped their mothers to cook the family meal.

In the 1860s, women and girls made almost everything the family ate. They cooked in an iron pot hanging over the flames in the open fireplace. They baked in a cast-iron camp oven that sat directly on top of the fire. Country families grew a lot of their own food or caught animals in the bush. Many had a vegetable patch, chickens, fruit trees and a cow or a goat. Mothers baked fresh bread or damper every day. They bought only the basics like tea, flour and sugar from the general store.

There was only one general store in most country towns. It stocked basic food items, clothes and household goods. As there weren't many towns, families relied on travelling salesmen, called hawkers, who rode around in large wagons. They sold pots and pans, fabric for making clothes, tools, medicines and special treats like toys. During the gold rushes, many Chinese families grew vegetables and sold them door to door.

Travelling salesmen sold goods to families in the bush.

In the country, boys learnt to shoot small birds and animals for their mothers to cook. Because there were no fridges, people had to eat food before it went bad. Everyone ate lots of bread and meat, washed down with strong, sweet tea. Even young children drank tea. Children sometimes had special treats like parrot pie and kangaroo stew, or sweet food such as puddings, fruit pies, cakes and boiled lollies.

A basic meal was bread, meat and strong, sweet tea.

White people often starved to death when they got lost in the bush, but Aboriginal people did not. They knew exactly where to find food and water. As toddlers, Aboriginal children learnt to identify their parents' tracks, to find native fruits, seeds and vegetables that were safe to eat, and to locate water. For example, in the Wimmera District they ate quandong berries, also known as wild peaches, and they got water from mallee trees by slicing into the roots and allowing the water to drip out.

Aboriginal people knew which food from the bush was safe to eat.

'Remember the eagle you saved from a snake, Ike? You were very brave!'

CHAPTER 4
Dingoes and Bushrangers

Sunday, 14 August 1864

'I'm still thirsty,' Frankie complained, as the children began yet another day's journey. They breakfasted on sweet grass stalks and drank rainwater that had collected in Isaac's hat. What a sorry sight they made as they limped along in their wet shoes, fighting their way through the scrub.

Their arms were scratched, their clothes were ripped and their hair was a tangled mess.

Isaac suddenly lashed out at the bushes with his stick. 'Why does this scrub all look the same!' he growled. 'Once we get home, I'm never going into the bush again!'

As the day warmed up, more creatures moved about in the scrub. Lizards of all shapes and sizes— stump-tailed, blue-tongued, bearded and legless—lazed in the sun and then scuttled away under the leaf litter when the children approached. A large goanna stared at them, until Frankie darted at it. It used its huge claws to run up the trunk of the closest tree.

'Frankie, don't go chasing things,' Jane snapped. 'The goanna could've run up you rather than that tree!'

Frankie's bottom lip trembled and a tear slipped down

Lizards of all shapes and sizes lazed in the sun.

his cheek. Jane hugged him tight. 'Come on,' she coaxed, 'I'll give you a piggyback.'

Isaac walked on ahead. Jane, staggering under Frankie's weight, made much slower progress. She was watching the ground when she bumped into Isaac. He was standing stock still, staring at the path ahead.

'What's wrong, Ike?' Jane whispered, as she gratefully lowered Frankie to the ground.

'A snake,' Isaac replied, pointing at a snake that was slithering sleepily across his path. The children stood very still while it went on its way. It was more interested in finding a warm rock to sun itself on than in biting anyone.

'Remember the eagle you saved from a snake, Ike?', Frankie asked. 'You were very brave!'

'Maybe I should kill this one too. We could eat it.'

'I'm not that hungry!' Jane said, making a funny face.

The weary travellers found a ring of saplings that created a leafy

*A snake was slithering
sleepily across Isaac's path.*

cave to sleep in for the night. It was just as well, for a heavy frost fell. Ice particles glittered in the moonlight as the children lay close together under Jane's thin dress. They were so tired they did not stir even when a dingo passed by, eyed them hungrily and then trotted off into the night, howling mournfully.

A dingo passed by, eyed the children hungrily and then trotted off into the night.

The bushmen in the search party happily gave up their day of rest on that Sunday. They scoured the scrub, but still did not find any tracks. Meanwhile, Hannah Duff, keeping a lonely vigil in the hut in case the children found their way home, was beginning to think she would never see them again.

Monday, 15 August 1864

Awoken by the enthusiastic screeching of a flock of green parrots, Isaac sat bolt upright, his face still bleary with sleep. Jane and Frankie lay on the ground, wide-eyed, but not yet properly awake.

'What are they so happy about?' Isaac grumbled.

'They're home,' Jane replied glumly, as she hauled herself to her feet and got dressed. 'How many days is it now, Ike? Surely Father must find us soon!'

Isaac counted on his fingers. 'It's four, I think.'

The children were awoken by the enthusiastic
screeching of a flock of green parrots.

'It feels like more than that!'

'What's for breakfast? Has Father come yet?' Frankie was now wide awake.

'Nothing and no,' Isaac said bluntly. Frankie's face dropped.

On they tramped, following the faint trails made by kangaroos, wallabies and other small animals.

'Yes!!!' Isaac suddenly yelled. 'We've found the broombush patch!'

Jane shrieked with excitement. 'Then, we'd better pick some broombush for Mother.'

The thought of home gave them some much-needed energy, and soon they had three large bundles of broombush tucked under their arms.

'Let's go. Mother and Father will be so happy to see us!' whooped Isaac as he charged off, running up a slope. 'Come on, you two, keep up, we're nearly home!' They ran after him, huge grins on their grubby faces.

But when Isaac came out of the broombush grove he stopped abruptly. There was no sign at all of their little hut and the parents they missed so much.

Isaac angrily threw his broombush on the ground. He sat on a log, a scowl on his face. Jane and Frankie both burst into tears.

'It's all my fault!' Isaac berated himself. He lashed out at some nearby wattle trees with his tomahawk. Then, feeling embarrassed about his outburst, he picked up the branches and whittled their ends to make new walking sticks for them all.

It was a very despondent trio that set off again, leaning on their sticks, heads bowed, feet dragging.

'Let's do something to take our mind off things,' Jane suggested, trying to lift Isaac's mood.

'Let's play bushrangers!' said Frankie enthusiastically. 'I'll be the goodie!'

'Okay,' Isaac agreed reluctantly. 'You be the brave policeman on your horse, Jane can be the fine lady in the mail coach and I'll be Mad Captain Melville.'

'Let's play bushrangers!'

Isaac hid in the bushes and jumped out as Jane pranced by, her head held regally, a wattle branch held like a parasol over her shoulder. 'Bail up!' he demanded. 'Give me your jewels and valuables!'

Jane cowered away from him and screamed, 'Help! Help! It's that dastardly villain Captain Melville.'

'I'll save you,' Frankie cried. And he galloped into the clearing and shot the bushranger dead. Isaac sprawled on the ground, staring into the sky.

'Do you think we should've just stayed in the one place and waited until someone found us, Jane?'

'That doesn't matter now. We just have to keep going.' She held out her hand and helped him up.

In the evening, they lay awake for a while, talking about Captain Melville's missing treasure, before finally drifting off into a fitful sleep.

That Monday morning, the searchers had gathered once more at Spring Hill Station.

'Not much chance of findin' them little ones alive, I reckon. Weather's gunna get 'em,' a bushman muttered to his mate.

'I know, but we've gotta keep lookin' till we find 'em. Their father won't ever give up.'

Later that day they found two small boot marks clearly visible in the sandy soil, and suddenly they had reason to hope.

'They've found some tracks, Boss,' the station manager informed Dugald Smith, the owner of Spring Hill Station, who had just joined the search. Dugald organised an emu walk, and soon a line of men advanced through the scrub, not shifting their eyes from the ground. Over the course of the day, they followed the track for many long miles through the dense bush, looking for signs of the children's presence.

'Tough little blighters, your children,' Dugald commented to John Duff. 'They just never give up.'

Two cooees, shouted close together, rang out.

'Sounds like someone's found something,' Dugald said.

Dugald Smith and John Duff rode towards the sound. They came upon a man standing in a clearing, something white held aloft in his hand. John Duff leant down and grabbed the tiny item. 'Socks! Frankie's socks! Why would he throw away his socks?'

'I've no idea,' said Dugald Smith, shaking his head. 'But we better camp here tonight. We don't want to lose the trail.'

And so they put their billies on the fire, ate meat and damper, and drank strong, sweet tea. Then they wrapped themselves in possum rugs and settled down for the night. All except John Duff, who sat staring into the dying fire, a small white sock held against his cheek.

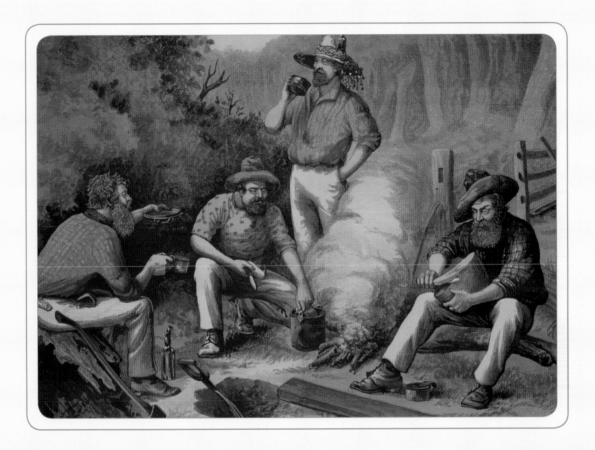

*The men put their billies on the fire, ate meat
and damper, and drank strong, sweet tea.*

SHANKS'S PONY, GOAT CARTS AND VELOCIPEDES: TRANSPORT IN THE 1860s

Some children had their own goat or dog cart.

There were no cars or planes in the 1860s. People had to get from one place to another by walking ('shanks's pony') or by riding a horse. Families who could afford it owned a cart, wagon or carriage. When they were little, children in wealthy families had beautifully carved and painted rocking horses. As they grew older, they drove carts pulled by a dog or a goat. Finally they were allowed to drive a carriage pulled by a horse.

Most children who lived in the bush learnt to ride horses at an early age. Often three or four of them would scramble onto the back of a horse and ride it to school or around the farm. In those days bicycles were big awkward things called velocipedes that only men could ride. Riders had to run alongside and then leap onto the seat.

Velocipedes were big, awkward bikes that only men could ride.

To go on a long trip, families caught a horse-drawn Cobb & Co. coach. These coaches travelled between major towns, carrying passengers, mail and newspapers. Travelling in a coach wasn't comfortable as it was hot, dusty, crowded and bumpy. And sometimes it was dangerous, because bushrangers often ambushed the coaches, stealing the mail and the passengers' valuables.

People travelled between towns in crowded, bumpy coaches.

Bullock drays (wagons) moved heavy goods and building materials around the countryside. Steam trains, paddle steamers, boats and coaches also carried freight. These different types of transport carried passengers from place to place, as well. The coaches and trains provided important communication links between towns and cities, and allowed families to keep in touch across the vast continent of Australia.

Trains carried both people and goods around the countryside.

In the strange light, the trees took on grotesque shapes and threatening silhouettes.

CHAPTER 5
Ants in the Pants and Packhorses

Tuesday, 16 August 1864

'Red sky at night, shepherd's delight; red sky in the morning, shepherd's warning,' Isaac chanted, as he lay on the hard earth, staring at a patch of sky winking at him through fluttering leaves. It was a threatening kaleidoscope of grey and red.

The three wanderers had no plan. They just mechanically followed the easiest path through the drab mallee scrub. Sometimes the landscape seemed familiar, but that was because they kept crossing their earlier tracks.

The quiet of the bush was suddenly shattered by screams.

'Make them stop! They're biting me!' Frankie yelled hysterically, jumping up and down and slapping wildly at his legs.

Isaac yanked him off an ants' nest. Then he pulled Frankie's pantaloons off him and used them to whack at the ants on the little boy's legs.

'Get them off! They hurt!' Frankie bawled, hopping on one foot and then the other.

'That was silly, getting ants in your pants! Keep still or we won't get them all,' said Jane, smiling despite Frankie's distress. A few minutes later, she carefully folded the tattered pantaloons and wrapped them in her kerchief.

'I'll take them home for Mother to mend. Look at your legs!'

Large red lumps announced where the ants had been and, in between them, there was a maze of cuts, grazes and bruises. Frankie started scratching at the bites, but Jane caught his hand to stop him.

'Those ants hurt me, Ike!' said Frankie, a tremor in his voice.

At that, Isaac lost his temper. He grabbed his walking stick and attacked the anthill, scattering the soil and killing ants as he slashed and stomped and ranted.

'Leave my brother alone, you rotters! Leave him alone!' Then Isaac slumped to the ground, his head in his hands. 'I don't think I can go any further.'

'Yes, you can. We're not going to get home without you,' Jane told him. Isaac, trying hard to be positive, stood up and then held out a hand to Frankie.

'Come on, wounded soldier, I'll give you a ride.'

A smile lit up Frankie's grubby face. 'You can be my packhorse,' he said as he heaved himself onto his big brother's back.

Isaac grimaced under the extra weight, but he set off at a slow trot.

'Giddy-up, horsie,' Frankie shouted. 'We've got to get the gold to the bank!'

Despite his exhaustion, Isaac got into the spirit of Frankie's game. 'When we get home we'll sell the gold and become rich. Mother shall have a new dress of blue velvet. Jane shall have a gorgeous porcelain doll. Father shall have the finest tobacco for his pipe. And I shall have that mechanical soldier the hawker showed us.'

'What about me?'

'Why, Frankie, you shall have a dappled rocking horse that will carry you to whatever magical place you desire!'

Frankie sighed and laid his head on Isaac's shoulder. 'Will it take me home?'

They stopped walking early that day, for another storm was coming.

'Joey Smith says that thunder is just God playing carpet bowls in the sky,' said Frankie, as thunder rumbled in the

The children stopped walking early that day, for another storm was coming.

distance. He snuggled in closer to Jane's back and drew her dress up to his chin.

The children lay wide-eyed in their bush bed while lightning unzipped the sky, illuminating everything with an eerie iridescence. In the strange light, the trees took on grotesque shapes and threatening silhouettes. And then the rain fell.

'That joey's got his mother. I want mine!'

John Duff was the first to rise that Tuesday morning. He quickly woke the others. Dugald Smith rallied the men, 'Come on, let's follow that trail! Horsemen at the front. Those on foot, keep your eyes peeled!'

Hope and enthusiasm buoyed them as they found more signs of the children's progress: whittled wood from the walking sticks Isaac had made, the withered wreath of flowers from Jane's bonnet and a bundle of broombush. With night descending, the men had to give up their search for the day. And with the darkness came the storm.

Wednesday, 17 August 1864

By the morning, the rain had stopped and the sun was out.

'Look, Jane, there's water everywhere. At least we've got plenty to drink!' said Isaac. After the children drank water from his hat, they stripped off their wet outer clothes and draped them over the surrounding bushes to dry. Lying in the early morning sunshine in their underwear, they watched steam rise from their garments into the morning air.

A flock of cockatoos screeched at one another as they hung upside down from the treetops and dried out their wings. A short way off a family of kangaroos grazed peacefully.

Frankie suddenly burst into tears.

'What's wrong?' Jane asked, patting his back.

'That joey's got his mother,' Frankie hiccupped, 'I want mine!'

When Frankie's sobbing had subsided, the children dressed and continued their aimless trekking. In the late afternoon they could go no further and, under a banksia bush, they fell into an exhausted sleep.

A flock of cockatoos screeched at one another.

The children could go no further and, under a banksia bush, they fell into an exhausted sleep.

'We were so close,' John Duff moaned, as darkness defeated the men once again.

'It's no good, mate,' the manager of Spring Hill Station said that frustrating Wednesday morning. 'The rain has washed away any sign of their tracks.' The men spent the day trying to pick up the children's trail again, but they did not have any luck.

'We were so close,' John Duff moaned, as darkness defeated them once again.

And, in the little hut on the edge of the mallee scrub, Hannah Duff looked out the window at the soggy bush, tears coursing down her cheeks. Hope had abandoned her.

BILBOQUETS, DISSECTIONS AND TANGRAMS:
CHILDREN'S TOYS IN THE 1860s

Children had a wide range of toys.

Children had a wide range of toys to play with in the 1860s. Fathers and sons from poor families constructed boxes, spinning tops, blocks, dolls houses, wheelbarrows and carts from wood and then painted them by hand. Mothers and daughters made balls from paper or rags stuffed with sawdust or wood shavings. Mothers also made dolls from wood, rags, hemp, straw and even handkerchiefs.

Wealthy families could afford to buy factory-made toys that came from Europe. Dolls with porcelain faces and mechanical or wind-up toys were very expensive. Parents bought them only on special occasions, such as birthdays or Christmas, and so children cherished these toys.

Girls loved their dolls with their fragile porcelain faces.

Most toys had an educational purpose. Girls had dolls, tea sets, dolls' houses, sewing sets, prams and toy shops to practise being mothers and housewives. Boys had tin soldiers, wooden guns, bows and arrows, and toy boats to develop skills that they'd need to get a job. Children also had toys just to have fun with, including hoops to roll along the ground, and a cup-and-ball game called bilboquet.

Hoops and skipping ropes were popular toys for outdoors.

Many of the toys that children played with in the 1860s are still popular: toys such as wooden animals, musical instruments, puppets, kites, marbles and shuttlecocks. Children loved jigsaws, which they called dissections, as well as tangram puzzles and rocking horses. They also got lots of outdoor exercise, riding on rickety tricycles and swinging on ropes tied onto tree branches.

Little boys liked riding on rocking horses and tricycles.

As evening set in, John Duff approached the camp and told the people of his children's plight.

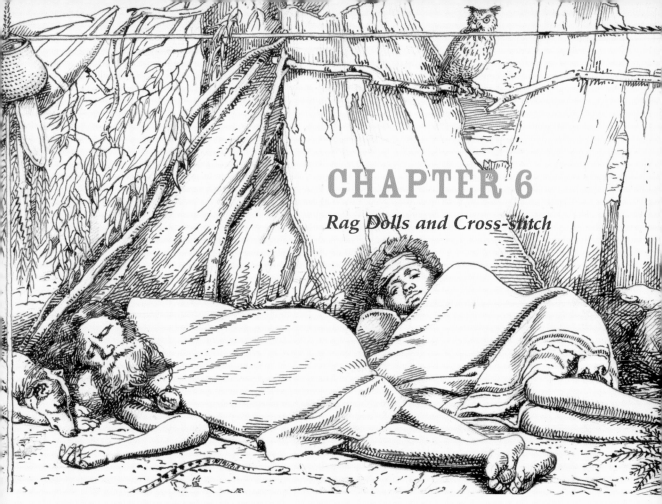

CHAPTER 6
Rag Dolls and Cross-stitch

Thursday, 18 August 1864

It was mid-morning when the children finally awoke. They were now too weak to cooee. Their voices were hoarse, their cheeks hollow and their eyes strangely bright.

'I can't walk,' Frankie croaked. Isaac picked him up, even though he hardly had the strength to carry himself.

'When you turn four, you'll be too big to carry,' Jane teased. Frankie poked his tongue out at her. It was a strange shade of yellow with what looked like fur growing on it. Jane wondered if hers looked the same.

On and on they staggered. They only stopped when Jane tripped over a log and lay sprawled on the ground. Accepting defeat, they crawled under a bush and fell asleep.

The searchers also felt defeated. No matter how hard they tried, they could not find the children's tracks. But John Duff would not give up.

'Where can we find some Aboriginal trackers?' he asked, as the men paused under a cypress pine.

'Well, mate, there's an Aboriginal group near Mount Elgin Station, but that's about 30 miles away. You won't get back here till tomorrow, and by then it might be too late.'

'Well, I have to do something!' the desperate father declared, mounting his horse and galloping away.

As evening set in, John Duff approached the camp and told the people of his children's plight.

'I'll help you look for your little ones,' declared Woorroral. 'My friends here will come too,' he said, pointing to two other men. 'But first you need to rest. We'll leave first thing tomorrow.'

Friday, 19 August 1864

'We have to get home,' Isaac wheezed. The wind smelt of yet more bad weather to come. Isaac, Jane and Frankie did not hear the cries of the birds as they flew wildly by, dipping and diving, for it took all their energy and concentration just to put one foot in front of the other.

The children didn't hear the cries of the birds as they flew wildly by.

Eventually, Frankie collapsed on the ground.

'Come on. We've got to find Father,' Jane moaned, brushing her lank hair out of her eyes. Bits of skin from her face stuck to her hand, but she did not notice.

'I'll carry Frankie,' Isaac whispered, but as he struggled to lift the little boy onto his back, his knees buckled and he fell flat on his face, with Frankie on top of him. It was some time before either of them moved.

Jane crawled over to them. 'Get up,' she rasped. And so they rallied once again. With Frankie in the middle, supported by his brother and sister, they lurched forward.

'Enough!' Jane finally groaned. They dropped to the ground like rag dolls and fell into a deep sleep, with no protection from the raging storm.

On that Friday morning, Alexander Wilson from Vectis Station joined the search party. He was a practised bushman and, to everyone's delight, he rediscovered the

children's tracks before the day was
too far advanced.

'Be careful, men,' he warned, 'it'll be
easy to lose the trail again.' And so they
progressed slowly, often on hands and
knees, throughout another long day. But
they did not find Isaac, Jane or Frankie.

Just as the storm reached its peak
in the early evening, John Duff and the
Aboriginal trackers caught up with the
search party. They had no choice but to huddle by the
campfire with the other men and wait till dawn.

*Tears flowed as Hannah Duff
gazed at the cross-stitch sampler
Jane had been making.*

At the little hut in the clearing, Hannah Duff sat fretting
over her children's belongings. She had them lined up on
the table—the boomerang Isaac had been carving, Jane's
rag doll and Frankie's favourite ball. Their mother had kept
a lonely vigil for seven long nights, hoping against hope to
hear the sound of her children's voices. Tears flowed as she
gazed at the cross-stitch sampler Jane had been making.

The alphabet was painstakingly sewn into the cloth in bright, cheerful colours.

'Now Jane will never learn to read a book,' Hannah sobbed, hugging Jane's doll to her chest.

Saturday, 20 August 1864

'Where am I?' Jane whispered, as she forced her eyes open. Against the odds, the three children had made it through yet another night. They were wet, hungry and confused. After thirstily sucking the moisture from their saturated clothes, they tried to walk, but after only a short distance all they could do was crawl.

'Stop … now!' Frankie demanded, collapsing on the ground.

'Just a little bit further. Please,' Isaac pleaded. The children dragged themselves on hands and knees into a natural chamber made of saplings, where fallen broombush provided a mattress and a wattle tree curtained them from the wind.

*Jane used the last of her energy to struggle out of her dress—the precious
dress that had been their only blanket for many cold nights.*

Jane used the last of her energy to struggle out of her
dress—the precious dress that had been their only blanket
for many cold nights. It was stained, torn and tattered.
As Jane drifted into sleep, her head against Frankie's
chest, she could hear his faint heartbeat, a quick and jerky
rhythm that was echoed by her own. Wrapped in one
another's arms, in what might well be their final place
of rest, they were unaware of the frantic search that was
going on not too far away.

Sometimes the trackers ran, sometimes they walked and sometimes they had to crawl.

As dawn broke that Saturday morning, only a handful of men remained in the search party, for provisions were low and many men had given up and returned home.

Woorroral and his companions started tracking the children. They could not only find tracks that no-one else could, but they could also read them like a book.

'Here the big one carried the little one,' Woorroral told John Duff. 'Here they slept in the scrub like baby birds in a nest, the littlest in the middle.'

Sometimes the trackers ran, sometimes they walked and sometimes they had to crawl, for the trail had been badly eroded by the heavy rain. With each clue they found and with each mile they covered, the searchers were more and more impressed by the children's tenacity.

'I can only pray we find them soon,' Alexander Wilson confided to Dugald Smith, 'for one thing is sure—they can't survive another night.'

SLATES, INKWELLS AND THE CANE:
SCHOOLING IN THE 1860s

Mothers often taught reading and writing at home.

Many children in the bush in the 1860s didn't go to school because there were very few schools. Also, schools charged fees and, at that time, attending school wasn't compulsory. Sometimes mothers or older brothers or sisters taught children to read, write and do basic arithmetic. Children from wealthy families also had lessons at home, but they had specially trained governesses who also taught them Latin, music, art and French.

In one-room schools, all the pupils were in the same class.

Some children went to bush schools. Teachers ran these schools either from their own houses or in huts made of hessian sacks and bark. There was only one classroom in a bush school and so children of all ages were together. The best students sat at the back of the class. Schooling was made compulsory in 1872 and new public schools with shiny corrugated-iron roofs and wooden walls replaced the bush schools.

If their parents worked on a farm, children often didn't go to school on days when they had to help with the harvesting or the shearing, or with the household chores. During the gold rushes, many children never went to school because they had to help their parents to search for gold. When they did go to school, children learnt grammar, reading, writing and arithmetic, and how to sew and knit.

Children didn't go to school when they had to help their parents.

Teachers emphasised punctuality, obedience, politeness and cleanliness, and they were very strict. They punished their pupils by slapping them or beating them with a cane or wooden ruler. Children learnt their lessons by rote, repeating in sing-song voices everything the teacher said. In the new public schools, children had pencils and slates, and inkwells and nib pens to write with. These schools also had blackboards, maps and charts. In those days, there were no computers, electronic whiteboards or libraries.

Students wrote with a pencil on a slate, or with nib pens and ink.

Oblivious to everything, they slept in their sapling bower while the frenzied search continued nearby.

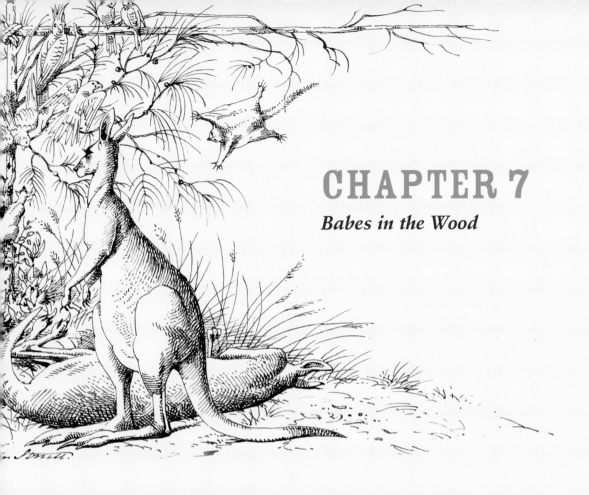

CHAPTER 7
Babes in the Wood

Saturday, 20 August 1864

'Mother,' Frankie murmured in his sleep, flinging an arm across Jane's body. Jane and Isaac did not stir. Oblivious to everything, they slept in their sapling bower while the frenzied search continued nearby.

'Over here!' Dugald Smith cried
out, late that afternoon. The searchers
anxiously gathered around him. 'Looks
like a fresh track just there, crossing
the one we've been following.'
Woorroral scanned the
ground. 'These were made
today. The children are alive!'
John Duff sank down onto
a log, his head in his hands.
'They're alive!' he whispered
in a voice full of wonder.
'Yes,' Woorroral continued,
'but they're in a bad way.
They can hardly stand.
They'll die soon, so we
must find them … now!'
And so the search
continued, Woorroral

'Looks like a fresh track just there.'

carefully checking each tiny sign. 'Here they were on hands and knees,' he announced. 'They're close.'

'I'll ride ahead. See if I can pick up the track further on,' John Duff said, unable to stand the slow pace any longer. And so he dropped the reins and let his horse have its head. The bay gelding arched its neck, snorted, then cantered through the bush for about a mile. And it was there that John Duff picked up the trail—a rut made in the sand by small boots. He cooeed twice and waited for the others to catch up.

'Here the big ones dragged the little one,' Woorroral declared.

To speed up the search, Alexander Wilson and John Duff took it in turns to ride ahead of the search party.

'It's nearly sunset. Where can they be?' John Duff was getting desperate.

The searchers anxiously gathered around.

Dugald Smith put a hand on his shoulder. 'We'll have to stop looking soon, John. We're running out of light.'

'No!' John Duff shouted, shrugging off Smith's hand. 'I'm not giving up now!' Then he pulled himself together. 'Sorry, Boss. But I have to keep looking. I'll just ride to the clump of saplings on that small rise over there. At least I'll get a better view.'

As he rode ahead, something pale caught his eye.

'What's that?' he asked himself. An evening breeze was blowing and something seemed to lift and stir amongst the saplings. John Duff spurred his horse forward.

And to John Duff's indescribable joy and unending amazement, he discovered his children.

And to his indescribable joy and unending amazement, he discovered his children, lying just like the fabled babes in the wood, their arms encircling each other. And Jane's dress was draped across all three of them.

John Duff whooped with joy and jumped from his horse. But the children did not stir, and he suddenly wondered whether he had arrived too late. Cautiously, he approached the small lifeless bodies and knelt beside them.

He brushed Jane's hair from her ravaged little face and bent to kiss her cheek. He felt the gentle flutter of her breath and let out a sigh of relief. Then he put his head on Isaac's chest. It rose and fell gently beneath him. Finally, he picked up Frankie's hand, and gasped as the small fingers grasped his own.

He sat beside his children, tears running down his cheeks. The other searchers caught up and started cheering and slapping one another on the back.

'We've found them!' The sounds of their jubilation finally woke first Isaac and then Frankie.

John Duff suddenly wondered whether he had arrived too late.

Isaac tried to sit up. His eyes glared wildly around then focused on his father's face. He tried to speak, but his mouth was so dry that all he could do was groan the word 'Father!' Then he collapsed back on the ground.

Frankie, whom Jane and Isaac had looked after as best they could, was in better shape. He looked John Duff directly in the eye and in his endearingly straightforward manner said, 'Father, why didn't you come for us sooner? We were cooeeing for you!'

And as for poor Jane, she was so ill that she did not even open her eyes when her father lifted her in his arms. She just curled into herself and murmured in a small tremulous voice, 'Cold! Cold!'

John Duff held her close. Then he placed her in Woorroral's arms while he rubbed her cold skinny little limbs. As some circulation returned, Jane stirred and opened her eyes. But when Woorroral saw how frightened she was at being in the arms of a total stranger, he gently passed the little girl back to her father. Jane gave the kind stranger a smile and snuggled into John Duff's chest.

'We must get them home straightaway,' Woorroral said firmly. 'They mustn't spend another night out here.'

And so the searchers gave the children what little food they had left—a small piece of bread and some ginger root—and gently trickled water from their pannikins into the children's mouths. Then, as darkness descended, they all set out on the final journey home.

At 8 o'clock on that glorious night, Hannah Duff heard the sound of horses approach her door. Running outside, she found the horsemen with their precious load. Many a tear was shed as she gathered her children into her arms. Home at last!

Many a tear was shed as Hannah Duff gathered her children into her arms. Home at last!

SAILOR SUITS, PINAFORES AND PANTALOONS: CHILDREN'S CLOTHING IN THE 1860s

Children had to wear formal, fancy clothes.

Life was much more formal in the 1860s than it is now. Children didn't wear t-shirts, board shorts or jeans, and they didn't go to big department stores or shopping malls to buy their clothes. Children's clothes were handmade and were much more complicated, multi-layered and uncomfortable. They had to dress like miniature adults, especially on Sundays when they wore their best clothes to church.

In the country, the women and girls made all the clothes. They bought fabric from travelling salesmen, who sold everything from cotton and silk to needles and thimbles. Mothers even made the lace used on collars and cuffs, and fathers carved buttons from wood, or used shell or glass. Wealthy families used seamstresses or maids to do the sewing, or imported their clothes from Europe.

Mothers made the family's clothes, including lace collars.

Girls wore dresses that came to the top of their heavy lace-up boots. They couldn't run or climb very easily in these outfits and they got very hot in summer. The clothes forced girls to behave in a 'ladylike' way. They wore large straw hats or bonnets to protect their 'delicate complexions' from the sun, and they put on Holland pinafores—white aprons with armholes—to keep their dresses clean. Under their dresses they had petticoats, long underwear called pantaloons and stockings held up by garters.

Girls had to wear dresses, petticoats and pantaloons.

Both little boys and girls usually wore the same clothes—dresses, petticoats and pinafores. When boys were about six, they got their first pair of short trousers, and at 14 they began to wear long trousers. Boys from wealthy families favoured sailor suits, knickerbockers (trousers that reached just below the knees), jackets and suits. Boys often rolled up their sleeves and didn't wear shoes in summer, but girls weren't allowed to go barefoot.

Little boys often wore dresses and pants decorated with lace.

EPILOGUE

Isaac, Jane and Frank Duff had walked nearly 100 kilometres over the nine days that they were lost. When they were found, they were suffering from exposure, dehydration and malnutrition.

Their mother, who was a midwife, nursed them back to health, with expert advice from members of the search party Alexander Wilson and Dugald Smith. A doctor, Archibald Macdonald, visited them on the Sunday after they were found, but there was no hospital nearby for them to be taken to. After three days, they were able to walk a little, but they were easily worn out and still very ill. It took them at least a month to recover from their ordeal.

The newspapers were very interested in their story, especially in the way Jane had acted like a 'little mother', looking after her brothers and covering them with her dress.

Isaac and Jane were Frank's half-brother and half-sister as their mother, Hannah Cooper, was a widow with two small children when she married John Duff.

As news spread about the children's miraculous survival, a memorial fund was established to help them and, in particular, to reward Jane, who attracted most public sympathy. Enough money was raised to give them an education. Jane was sent to a boarding school some distance away called Mrs Bowden's Private School for Young Ladies.

When she was 19, Jane married George Turnbull, a bootmaker. They lived in Horsham and had 11 children. They named two of their boys Frank and Isaac. When Jane died in 1932 aged 75, she still had the dress that she had used to protect her brothers from the cold. She also had a Bible that had been sent to her by Tasmanian school children in honour of her 'heroism', and a small sculpture of her holding her little brother, which had been sent to her by an admirer in Britain.

The three Aboriginal trackers were rewarded by the station owner and by John Duff.

Isaac moved to the nearby town of Nhill in the 1890s, where he worked as a station hand. He married and had four children. He died in 1938. Frank moved to Queensland, where he married and had one son. Unfortunately, he lost touch with his siblings.

The three Aboriginal trackers who helped find the children were rewarded with £5 by the station owner and £10 by John Duff. As John Duff earned only £50 a year, this was a very generous reward. Woorroral, who was also known as Jungunjinanuke and King Richard, was a very good cricketer. He was a member of the Aboriginal cricket team which, in 1868, was the first Australian team to tour England.

A granite memorial was erected in 1935 to commemorate the children's survival. It can still be found in Jane Duff Highway Park on the road between Natimuk and Goroke in Victoria. Jane was buried in Horsham Cemetery, and the words 'Bush Heroine' are inscribed on her headstone.

BACKGROUND READING

The Story of the Duff Children

Blake, L.J., *Lost in the Bush: The Story of Jane Duff*. Melbourne: Whitcombe & Tombs, 1964.

Dodds, Peter (director), *Lost in the Bush*. Melbourne, Vic.: Film Unit, Audio Visual Education Centre, Victorian Department of Education, 1973.

'Loss and Apprehended Death of Three Children', *Hamilton Spectator*, vol. 10, 24 August 1864, p. 2.

Meagher, Beverley (comp.), *Women of Arapiles: Past and Present.* Natimuk: Shire of Arapiles, 1985.

Pierce, Peter, *The Lost Children: An Australian Anxiety.* Cambridge: Cambridge University Press, 1999.

Simpson, Patrick, 'The Story of the Lost Children', *Weekly Review and Messenger*, 10 September 1864, Supplement, pp. 1–2.

Strutt, William, *Cooey, or, The Trackers of Glenferry*. Canberra: National Library of Australia, 1989.

Torney, Kim, *Babes in the Bush: The Making of an Australian Image*. Fremantle, WA: Curtin University Books, 2005.

Victorian Readers Fourth Book. Melbourne: Education Department of Victoria, 1930.

Life in the 1860s

Blake, L.J. and K.H. Lovett (comp.), *Wimmera Shire Centenary: An Historical Account*. Horsham, Vic.: Wimmera Shire Council, 1962.

Cliff, Paul (ed.), *The Endless Playground: Celebrating Australian Childhood.* Canberra: National Library of Australia, 2000.

Dow, Gwyn and June Factor (eds), *Australian Childhood: An Anthology.* Ringwood, Vic.: McPhee Gribble, 1991.

Dugan, Michael, *The Golden Years 1850–1890*. Melbourne: Macmillan, 1997.

Fabian, Suzane and Morag Loh, *Australian Children through 200 Years*. Kenthurst, NSW: Kangaroo Press, 1985.

Guile, Melanie, *Bush Boys & Girls: Pioneer Children in the 1800s*. Port Melbourne, Vic.: Heineman Library, 2005.

Kociumbas, Jan, *Australian Childhood: A History*. St Leonards, NSW: Allen & Unwin, 1997.

LIST OF ILLUSTRATIONS

page 11
Nicholas Chevalier (1828–1902)
Mallee Scrub, Murray River, NSW
1871 (detail)
watercolour; 25.5 x 39.0 cm
Pictures Collection
nla.pic-an2962212

page 12
Nora Heysen (1911–2003)
Moodoobahngul 1930
pen and ink; 16.8 x 23.1 cm
Pictures Collection
nla.pic-an23217504

page 14, top
Illustration by Stephanie Owen
Reeder based on:
Nicholas Caire (1837–1918)
Hut Used for Winter Quarters 1884 (detail)
albumen photograph; 5.8 x 9.4 cm
Pictures Collection
nla.pic-an3096938-8

and
J. Chester Jervis
Group of Children outside a Building (School?)
(between 1860 and 1880) (detail)
albumen silver photograph; 18.0 x 22.8 cm
Pictures Collection
nla.pic-an6647839-53

page 14, bottom
John Godfrey (c.1817–1889)
Australian Shepherd's Hut 1874? (detail)
engraving; 19.5 x 26.5 cm
Pictures Collection
nla.pic-an7370537

page 15, top
Stanley Leighton (1837–1901)
*Killingoola, Mr. Seymour's nr. Penola, South
Australia, Sat. 24 Ap. 1868* (detail)
watercolour; 8.2 x 25.0 cm
Pictures Collection
nla.pic-an4620462

page 15, bottom
Emma Minnie Boyd (1856–1936)
*Bush Scene, the Walk: Chiltern
Area North-eastern Victoria, 1860s* c.1865
oil on gum leaf; 12.5 x 20.3 cm
Pictures Collection
nla.pic-an2263599

Chapter 2

page 54, top
Illustration by Stephanie Owen
Reeder based on:
William Henry Corkhill (1846–1936)
Norman Corkhill Aged about 4,
in a Goat Cart 1894
glass negative
Pictures Collection
nla.pic-an2438340

page 54, bottom
Samuel Calvert (1828–1913)
First Velocipede Race on the Melbourne
Cricket Ground 1869? (detail)
wood engraving; 22.5 x 37.7 cm
Pictures Collection
nla.pic-an10280445

page 55, top
Arthur Esam (1850–1934)
Royal Mail Coach, Hill & Co. 1890s
watercolour; 16.3 x 27.7 cm
Pictures Collection
nla.pic-an6621169

page 55, bottom
C. Haydon
Special Good Friday Religious Ceremony
Train on Camden Line ...
(between 1937 and 1950) (detail)
b&w photograph; 6.4 x 10.9 cm
Pictures Collection
nla.pic-an23252033

Chapter 5

page 56
William Strutt (1825–1915)
The Children at Night Watching a
Corroboree c.1876
pencil and wash; 22.3 x 27.9 cm
Pictures Collection
nla.pic-an3241549

page 57
William Strutt (1825–1915)
Illustration for Chapter 5 of the
Artist's Story Cooey ... c.1876
pen; 14.9 x 21.0 cm
Pictures Collection
nla.pic-an3241452

page 61
Edward Thomson (active 1840–1870)
Sydney Heads from Sea, Moonlight 1848? (detail)
watercolour; 17 x 32.4 cm
Pictures Collection
nla.pic-an4652153

page 62
William Strutt (1825–1915)
The Haunt of the Kangaroo 1885
watercolour; 48.0 x 88.6 cm
Pictures Collection
nla.pic-an3211954

page 64
William Strutt (1825–1915)
*Australian Parrots: Cockatoos,
Parakeets* c1860 (detail)
pencil and wash; 12.5 x 24.2 cm
Pictures Collection
nla.pic-an3259578

page 65
Ellis Rowan (1848–1922)
Banksia marginata, *Silver Banksia* c.1886
watercolour; 56 x 38 cm
Pictures Collection
nla.pic-an6724543

page 66
Millard Glendale
Settlers in the Australian Bush 1898 (detail)
oil on galvanised iron sheet; 61.0 x 91.0 cm
Pictures Collection
nla.pic-an2273970

page 67
Ellis Rowan (1848–1922)
Banksia prionotes 1880s (detail)
watercolour; 74.1 x 54.0 cm
Pictures Collection
nla.pic-an7677465

page 68, top
Illustration by Stephanie Owen
Reeder based on:
J. Chester Jervis
Three Children on a Porch
(between 1860 and 1880)
albumen silver photograph; 18.0 x 22.8 cm
Pictures Collection
nla.pic-an6647839-49

page 68, bottom
John Hubert Newman (1830–1916)
Portrait of Australia Little 1880s
sepia-toned photograph; 10.3 x 6.3 cm
Pictures Collection
nla.pic-an24156294

page 69, top
N. Smith (active 1845)
Portrait of Four Children ... Carrying Toys 1845
watercolour; 30.7 x 25.2 cm
Pictures Collection
nla.pic-vn3280961

page 69, bottom
Nicholas White (active 1875–1891)
*Portrait of Frederick Michael Thomas,
Aged 4 years* 1880s (detail)
sepia-toned photograph; 10.5 x 6.3 cm
Pictures Collection
nla.pic-an24154154

Chapter 6

page 81, bottom
E. Bayning
Book Study 1800s (detail)
oil on cardboard; 30.5 x 23.0 cm
Pictures Collection
nla.pic.an2291808

Chapter 7

page 82
William Strutt (1825–1915)
The Little Wanderers 1865
watercolour; 14.2 x 19.5 cm
Pictures Collection
nla.pic-an3240607

page 83
William Strutt (1825–1915)
*Illustration for Chapter 6 of the
Artist's Story* Cooey … c.1876
pen; 14.9 x 21.1 cm
Pictures Collection
nla.pic-an3241474

page 84
William Strutt (1825–1915)
*Study of First Bushranger for Bushrangers,
Victoria, Australia, 1852* 1886
pencil and wash; 52.7 x 36.3 cm
Pictures Collection
nla.pic-an3230644

page 85
William Strutt (1825–1915)
Swagman, and Woman c.1860 (detail)
pencil; 25.7 x 20.3 cm
Pictures Collection
nla.pic-an3211931

page 86
Samuel Thomas Gill (1818–1880)
The Duff Children, August 20, 1864 1864 (detail)
chromolithograph; 20.0 x 25.0 cm
Pictures Collection
nla.pic-an7149197

page 88
William Strutt (1825–1915)
*Found! Mr. Duncan, Roderick, Bella
and David* c.1876
pencil and wash; 15.0 x 19.2 cm
Pictures Collection
nla.pic-an3241592

page 91
William Strutt (1825–1915)
Home at Last c.1876
pencil and wash; 14.9 x 19.3 cm
Pictures Collection
nla.pic-an3241602

*Full images have been reproduced in this list
only where they were substantially cropped
or used as reference for illustrations.*